Walter Crane

A Floral Fantasy in an Old English Garden

Set Forth in Verses & Coloured Designs

Walter Crane

A Floral Fantasy in an Old English Garden
Set Forth in Verses & Coloured Designs

ISBN/EAN: 9783337072520

Printed in Europe, USA, Canada, Australia, Japan

Cover: Foto ©Andreas Hilbeck / pixelio.de

More available books at **www.hansebooks.com**

A FLORAL FANTASY
IN AN OLD ENGLISH
GARDEN
BY
WALTER CRANE

NEW YORK &
LONDON HARPER
AND BROTHERS

·A·FLORAL· ·FANTASY·

A FLORAL
FANTASY
IN AN OLD
ENGLISH
GARDEN

SET FORTH IN
VERSES & COL=
OURED DESIGNS
BY
WALTER CRANE

LONDON: AT THE
HOUSE OF HARPER
AND BROTHERS:
1899

THE OLD ENG·LISH GARDEN A FLORAL PHAN·TASY ✠ ✠ ✠

In an old·world· garden dreaming,
Where the flowers had human names,
Methought, in fan· tastic seeming,
They disported as squires and dames.

O fold in Rosamond's
Bower,
With its peacock hedges
of yew,
One could never find
the flower
Unless one was given
the clue;
So take the key of the
wicket,
Who would follow my
fancy free,
By formal knot and
clipt thicket,
And smooth green-
sward so fair to see

And while Time
his scythe
is whetting,
Ere the dew
from the grass
has gone,

The Four
   Seasons'
        flight
forgetting,
As they dance
round the
    dial stone;

With a leaf
from an old
English book.
A JONQUIL
will serve for
a pen.

Let us note
from the green
arbour's nook,

Flowers mask-
ing like women
and men

FIRST in
VENUS'S
LOOKING
GLASS,

You may see
where

LOVE LIES
BLEEDING,

11

While
PRETTY
MAIDS

all of them pass

With careless
hearts quite un
heeding.

Next, a knight
with his flam-
ing targe
See the
DENT-DE-LION
so bold
With his feath-
ery crest at large,
On a field of the
cloth of gold.

Simple Honesty
shows in vain
A fashion few
seek to robe in,
While the poor
SHEPHERD'S PURSE
is ta'en
By rascally
RAGGED ROBIN.

COLTSFOOT
and
LARKSPUR

SPEEDWELL

15

In the race
of the flowers
that's run
             due.

As the
HARTSTONGUE
pants
at the well

And the
HOUNDSTONGUE
laps the
SUNDEW.

Here's
VENUS·COMBE
for
MAIDENHAIR:
While
KING·CUPS
drink
BELLA·DONNA.

Clad in purple
and gold
so fair,
Though the
DEADLY
NIGHTSHADE's
upon her.

Behold
LONDON PRIDE
robed & crowned,
Ushered in by the
GOLDEN ROD,
While a floral
crowd press
around,
Just to win from
her crest a nod.

The Foxgloves
are already on,
Not only in pairs
but dozens;
They've come out
to see all the fun,
With sisters and
aunts
and cousins.

The
STITCHWORT
looked up
with a sigh

At
BATCHELOR'S
BUTTONS
unsewn:

Single Daisies
were not
in her eye,

For
the grass
was just
newly mown.

The HORSE-
TAIL,
'scaped from
WOLFE'S CLAW,
Rides off with
a LADIES' LACES.

The FRIAR'S·
COWL
hides
a doctor of law,
And the
BISHOPS·WEED
covers
     his grace's

The
SNAPDRAGON
opened his jaw,
But, at sight of
Scotch
THISTLE,
turned pale :

He 'd
too many points
of the law

For a dragon
without
a scale .

Little JENNY-
GREEPER
lay low,
Till happy thoughts
made her gladder;
How to rise in the
world she'd know,
So she climbed up
JACOB'S LADDER

SWEET WILLIAM
with
MARYGOLD
Seek
HEARTSEASE
in the close box-
border,
Where, starched
in their ruff's stiff
fold
DUTCH DAHLIAS
prim, keep order.

NARCISSUS
bends over the
brook,

Intent upon
DAFFA·DOWN·
DILLY:

While EYEBRIGHT
    observes from
        her nook,
And wonders he
    could be so
        silly.

A LANCE FOR
A LAD 'gainst
KING'S SPEAR,
when the BUGLE
sounds for
the play

A LADIES MANT-
LE flaunting
there
Is the banner
that leads
the fray.

KNIGHT'S SPUR
to the
LADIES BOWER
to seek for the
LADIES SLIPPER.

'T was lost in
the wood
in a summer
shower
When the
CLOWN'S WORT
tried to trip her.

TOAD-FLAX
is spun
for
BUTTER-
AND-EGGS

On a LADIES'
CUSHION sits
THRIFT
She never wastes,
  or steals, or begs,
But she can't give
  poor RAGWORT
  a lift.

QUEEN OF
THE MEADS
is MEADOWSWEET,
In the realm
of grasses
wide:

But not in
   all her court
you meet
The turbaned
TURK'S HEAD
in his pride.

Fair BETHLEHEM'
STAR
shineth bright,

In a lowly
place, as
of old,

And through
the green gloom
glows the light

of ST. JOHN'S
WORT - a
nimbus of gold.

But the hours
of the sun
swift glide,

And the flowers
with them are
speeding.

Though
LOVE-IN-A-MIST
may hide,

When Time's in
the garden
weeding.

There's TRAVELLER'S JOY To entwine, At our journey's end for greeting,

We can
    talk over
Sops-in-Wine,
And drink to
    our next
merry meeting.

www.ingramcontent.com/pod-product-compliance
Lightning Source LLC
Chambersburg PA
CBHW021233260626
47172CB00002B/749